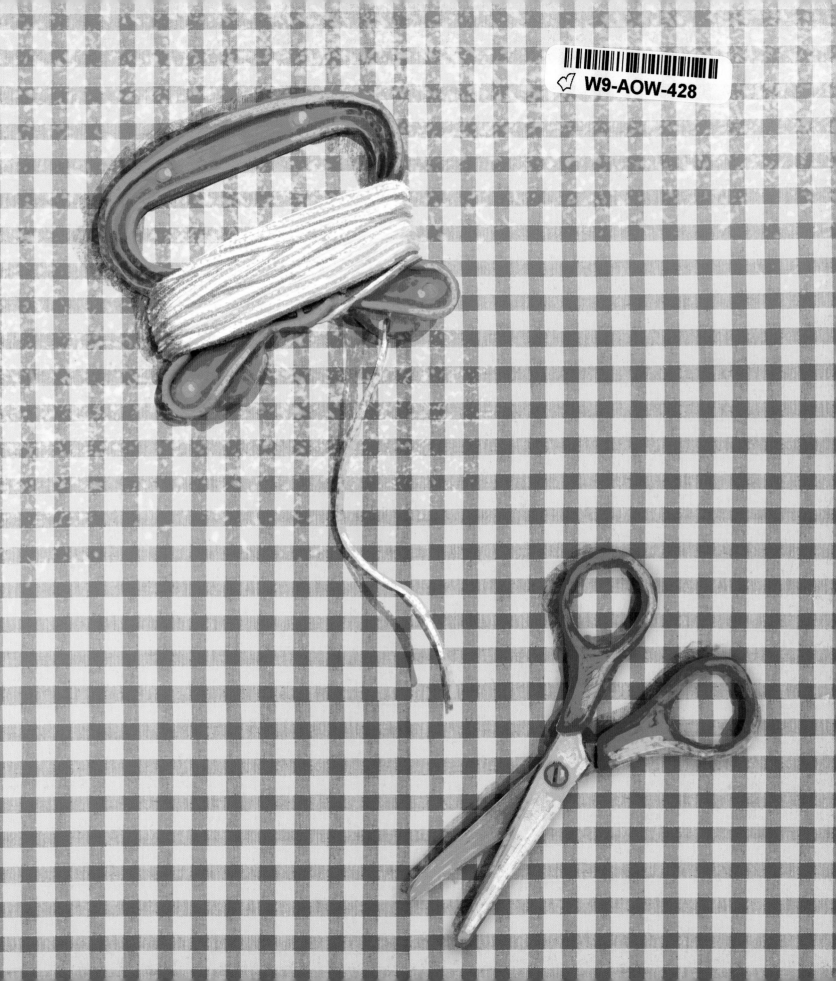

This book is dedicated to children everywhere.

Be kind to each other.

Visit us on the Web at www.clavisbooks.com.

Benji and The Giant Kite written by Alan C. Fox and illustrated by Eefje Kuijl

ISBN 978-1-60537-403-1

This book was printed in April 2018 at Publikum d.o.o., Slavka Rodica 6, Belgrade, Serbia.

First Edition
10 9 8 7 6 5 4 3 2 1

www.alancfox.com
www.eefjekuijl.com

BENJI &
THE GIANT KITE

Clavis
NEW YORK

Alan C. Fox & Eefje Kuijl

Benji loved purple skies, sunset skies, cloudy skies, blue skies, and kite skies.

Especially kite skies.

Benji often spent his allowance at the local toy store
for a kite and twine.

Benji lived near a beach where a strong wind blew.
It was a great wind for kite flying. But sometimes,
just when his kite became a speck in the summer sky,
the wind would suddenly drop, and so would his kite.
Benji had lost many kites on that beach.

One day the man at the store suggested a box kite.
Benji couldn't believe a kite shaped like a box could fly.
But Benji liked new ideas.

On it's very first flight,
the box kite crashed into a tree.
Benji cried.

The next time Benji's mom took him to the toy store
he saw a giant, diamond-shaped kite.
It was much bigger than the other kites.
Benji wanted that kite.
"Mom, this is a really nice kite."
"I'm sorry, dear, but you've already spent your allowance."

"I'll weed the garden?"
"All right. But we'll have
to put the kite away
until you earn
the money."

Benji worked in the garden for two weeks. In the morning he weeded the vegetables.
In the afternoon he weeded the flower beds.
It seemed he would never finish. But Benji wanted that kite,
so he worked hard.

Finally, Benji's mom took the kite out of the closet. "You did a good job, Benji," she said.

Benji held the kite gently so it wouldn't break
on the way to the beach.

He ran over the sand to the sea.
The kite tugged gently at the twine and then floated into the air
like a dandelion seed.

Benji's giant kite soared higher and higher with every gust of air.
It rose over all the people.
It rose over the hotdog stand and the houses beyond.
The kite turned right and left at Benji's command. He was a kite whisperer.

Benji let his little brother hold the twine, and his father, too.
At last the giant kite had drawn all of the twine toward the clouds.
The kite was just a distant speck in the sky.

"Time to go," said Benji's dad.
"Let's bring your kite home."
Benji looked up at his giant kite flying
near the clouds where it belonged.

He breathed the freshness of the evening air
and for one final moment felt the kite tugging on the twine in his hand.
Before he could change his mind, Benji unwound the twine and let it go.
"Goodbye, kite," Benji said.

He fixed that moment in his memory,
and then turned to leave as the giant orange kite
floated free into the sunset sky.

IT MAY BE UP THERE YET.